KU-022-155

This book belongs to

....

....

PUFFIN BOOKS

UK | USA | Canada | Ireland | Australia | India | New Zealand | South Africa

Puffin Books is part of the Penguin Random House group of companies whose
addresses can be found at global.penguinrandomhouse.com

First published by Ladybird Books 2004
This edition published by Puffin Books 2017
001

Copyright © the Eric and Gillian Hill Family Trust, 2004

The moral right of the author/illustrator has been asserted

Manufactured in China

A CIP catalogue record for this book is available from the British Library

ISBN: 978–0–241–32646–6

All correspondence to:
Puffin Books, Penguin Random House Children's
80 Strand, London, WC2R 0RL

Time for Bed,
Spot

Eric Hill

It was getting late. Spot had
finished his supper. Now he was
busy playing with his train,
his blocks and his ball.

Sally looked in.
"Time for bed, Spot," she said.
"But, Mum," said Spot,
"I'm not sleepy!"

"You can tidy up your toys,"
said Sally. "That will help to
make you sleepy."
"All right, Mum," said Spot.

He put away his train,
his blocks and his ball.

"I'm still not sleepy!" said Spot.

"A nice warm bath will help,"
said Sam, Spot's dad.

He filled the bath with lovely
warm bubbles for Spot.
Spot stayed in the bath for a long
time, playing with his boat
and his duck.

But, when it was time to come out, Spot still wasn't sleepy – not even when Sam wrapped him in a big, fluffy towel!

"I'll read you a story," said Sally.
"That will send you off to sleep."

Sally read Spot his favourite story. It was all about pirates and their adventures on the high seas.

"Read it again, please," said Spot, when she had finished.

So Sally read the story again.
"Thanks, Mum," said Spot.
"Maybe I can go to sleep now."

"Just close your eyes and
you'll soon drift into
dreamland," said Sally.

Spot closed his eyes and Sally kissed him goodnight. Then she tiptoed out of the room.

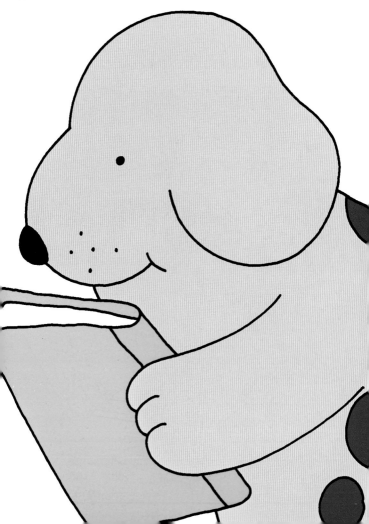

But Spot STILL wasn't sleepy!

"I can't stay in bed when I'm not sleepy," he said to himself. "I'll get up and pretend to be a pirate, like the ones in my storybook."

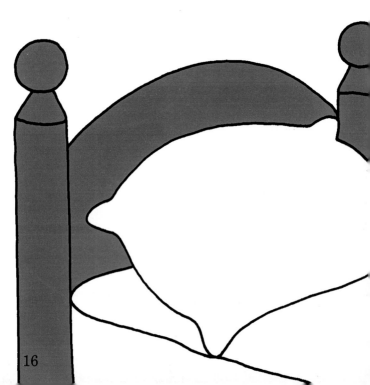

Spot went to his dressing-up
cupboard. He got out an eye patch,
a bandana and a wooden sword.

"Yo-ho-ho!" he said, jumping up and down. "I'm the pirate king of the high seas!"

After a while, Spot got tired of being a pirate. But he still wasn't sleepy!

"I'll pretend to be something else now," he said, looking in his dressing-up cupboard. "What will I be?"

"I'll be a cowboy!" Spot decided.

He put on his cowboy hat and he found his horse. Spot rode his horse all around the room. Stomp! Stomp! Stomp!

"I'm a buckaroo!" he shouted.
"This is so much fun – it's a good
thing I'm not sleepy!"

Sally came to the door.

"You're supposed to be asleep!" she called. "What's all the noise about?"

But Spot didn't answer.

25

That's because Spot didn't hear her. He was curled up in his dressing-up clothes – fast asleep!

Sally picked up Spot and tucked him into bed.

"I think I was sleepy after all, Mum," he murmured.

"I think you were," said Sally,
smiling. She gave Spot a hug and
another goodnight kiss.
"Sweet dreams, Spot! Sleep tight!"

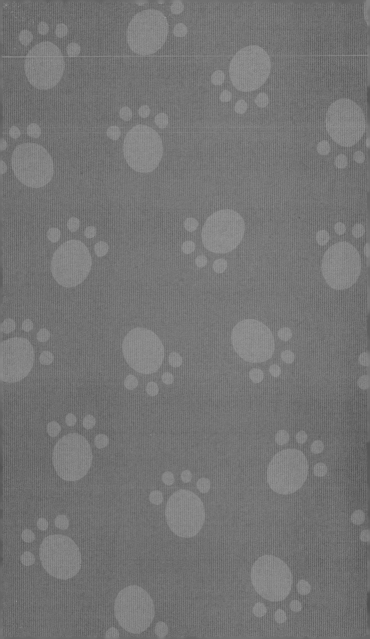